Bantam Books in the Choose Your Own Adventure® Series
Ask your bookseller for the books you have missed.

THE MONA LISA IS MISSING!

BY RAMSEY MONTGOMERY

An R. A. Montgomery Book

ILLUSTRATED BY GONZALEZ VICENTE

BANTAM BOOKS
TORONTO • NEW YORK • LONDON • SYDNEY • AUCKLAND

RL 4, IL age 10 and up

THE MONA LISA IS MISSING!
A Bantam Book / February 1988

CHOOSE YOUR OWN ADVENTURE® is a registered trademark of
Bantam Books. Registered in U.S. Patent and Trademark
Office and elsewhere.

Original conception of Edward Packard
Cover art by James Warhola
Inside illustrations by Gonzalez Vicente

ISBN 0-553-27004-4

Published simultaneously in the United States and Canada

Bantam Books are published by Bantam Books, a division of Bantam
Doubleday Dell Publishing Group, Inc. Its trademark, consisting of the
words "Bantam Books" and the portrayal of a rooster, is Registered in
U.S. Patent and Trademark Office and in other countries. Marca Regis-
trada. Bantam Books, 666 Fifth Avenue, New York, New York 10103.

PRINTED IN THE UNITED STATES OF AMERICA

O   0 9 8 7 6 5 4 3 2 1

THE MONA LISA
IS MISSING!

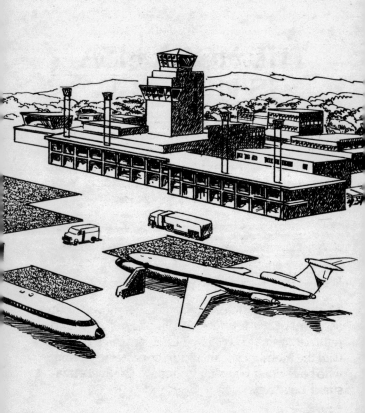

WARNING!!!

Do not read this book straight through from beginning to end! These pages contain many different adventures you may have when the famous *Mona Lisa* is stolen and you're assigned to the case by the French FBI. From time to time, as you read along, you will be asked to make a choice. Your choice may lead to success or disaster.

The adventures you have are the result of your choice. You are responsible because you choose! After you make your choice, follow the instructions to see what happens to you next.

Think carefully before you make a move. Your assignment, to find the missing *Mona Lisa* and return it to the Louvre, will bring you face to face with the members of an international terrorist ring, who have other plans for Leonardo da Vinci's treasured painting!

Good luck!

Mona Lisa Stolen!

PARIS, 15 March

In Paris yesterday, thieves broke into the Louvre museum and stole the famous *Mona Lisa*. Police investigating the crime have no substantial clues. It is suspected that the recent rash of terrorist bombings, including the bombing of the central post office three days ago, is in some way connected to the theft. For several days the Louvre has been protected by only a third of its regular guards, since additional men and women have been needed to cover government buildings. It is rumored that the Sûreté is bringing in an American specialist to help with the case. . . .

Turn to page 2.

You can't believe it; just two weeks before your family's scheduled visit to Paris, the *Mona Lisa* has been stolen! You toss the newspaper you were reading onto the coffee table and sink down on a chair in the living room. Seeing the *Mona Lisa* was to be the high point of your trip. But even though you're greatly disappointed by the theft, you've always been interested in crimes involving art, and the disappearance of the famous painting promises to be a particularly intriguing case.

Turn to page 6.

You grab Sergeant Schnitzler and drag him into the woods and then to the car. The men are busy trying to shoot Kurt. By sheer luck, the three of you reach your car and manage to get inside. Driving down the road at top speed, you wonder if retreat is the right thing.

"Let's go back," you say.

Kurt just laughs. "You Americans are always so courageous. If you want to be shot, return." He slows down.

"Who were they?" you ask.

"Thieves, terrorists, madmen. Who knows? The world is full of them these days. 'Stay alive,' that's my motto."

Schnitzler is taken to a hospital, and you and Kurt return to police headquarters. There you're met with the news that you've been removed from the case.

"Why?" you ask.

"Political reasons, political reasons," is the frustrating answer.

The *Mona Lisa* is never found.

The End

4

Pierre leaves reluctantly, but you feel that some-one must stay and watch the hut. You creep in even closer, and can just barely hear what the men inside are saying.

"Clive, you go back to Saas-Fee and get the painting from the hotel," says one.

You move closer. You crouch just under a win-dow at the back of the hut.

"When we reach Zermatt," says another voice, "we will take the cable cars into Italy where we will be safe."

The door to the hut opens and you flatten your-self against the wall. When you dare to peek around, you see the man you followed to the hut. He's hiking back down the trail to Saas-Fee.

Once again you follow him at a distance. You've got to beat him back to the hotel and somehow catch him with the painting. You veer off the trail and into the woods, and end up ahead of the man.

"Hallo! Hallo! What are you doing up here?" he yells to you.

Turn to page 64.

The decision not to work with Pierre is a tough one, but you feel that it's for the best. You step out into the reception area where your friend is waiting and give him the bad news. He takes it well.

"I understand," he says. "After all, the *Mona Lisa* is at stake."

Back in Mme. Delavoix's office, you discuss two possibilities based on evidence that the Sûreté has gathered. Some of their sources believe that the painting will be flown from Paris to London on a late-night flight, while other sources indicate that it will be flown to Jersey, a small island between France and England.

Mme. Delavoix indicates that the choice of which lead to follow is yours to make. "Whatever you decide, our agents Frederic and Dominique will be with you. Several of our other agents can check out the other leads, including Pierre's," she adds.

If you choose to take the flight to London, turn to page 10.

If you choose to take the flight to Jersey, turn to page 16.

6

Two days later, you find yourself in Orly, one of the airports in Paris. The theft of the *Mona Lisa* has dramatically changed your plans. Right after you finished reading about the theft, you received a telephone call from the Sûreté (France's FBI) asking for your help in recovering the painting. This came as something of a surprise to you, even though you had received a lot of publicity when you helped locate a stolen painting in Washington, D.C., a year ago. Your inventive and unique solution to that case brought much attention in the press, and now you're internationally known.

Even so, it's hard to believe that you're the "American specialist" mentioned in the newspaper report. As you board the métro, the Paris subway, that's departing from the airport, you think about how you'll present yourself to the world-famous Sûreté during your five-o'clock meeting later today.

You get off the subway at a stop in the center of Paris, right next to the apartment building where your good friend Pierre lives. You've arranged to stay with Pierre while you're in Paris.

Turn to page 9.

"We never stole the *Mona Lisa*," the smuggler responds nervously. "But we did sell two copies in France. You were to deliver them."

"Well, I guess the *Mona Lisa* is lost for now, but at least we found these," you say, pointing to a Picasso and a Rembrandt.

The paintings are returned to their owners, and you and Pierre are given large rewards, but the *Mona Lisa* is never found.

What a shame, you think years later when you're the curator of a famous art gallery in Washington, D.C. Of all the paintings in the world I wanted to see, the one I most wanted to see was the *Mona Lisa*.

The End

As you approach his building, your excitement increases. You haven't seen Pierre in over a year, not since he was an exchange student in the United States at your school. Pierre's not only a good friend, but he was a help to you in the Washington, D.C., case. You're hoping he can help you again. His interest in politics has given him many underground connections. He can often gain information about terrorist activities.

Pierre isn't at home, but he's left the keys to his apartment with the concierge. You let yourself in and look around. Stuck to the refrigerator you find a note: "Welcome! I am working at a small café called the Saint Robert. Meet me there. It is on the Champs Élysées. Before you leave, please listen to the answering machine for any change in plans."

Great, you think, I'll be able to get in a bit of sightseeing on the way to the café.

You switch on the answering machine. The first message is one you didn't expect. It's from Madame Daphne Delavoix, the head of the Sûreté, asking you to meet her at three-thirty instead of at five, if possible. It's already two o'clock. The second message is from Pierre. He says that he has some important information and asks you to meet him on the top level of the Eiffel Tower between three and four o'clock. Both messages sound important. You know you must act quickly.

If you decide to see Pierre first,
turn to page 70.

If you think you should see Mme. Delavoix
immediately, turn to page 89.

The flight to London is absolutely uneventful. You, Frederic, and Dominique see no one suspicious on board, and as far as you can tell, no paintings are loaded onto or removed from the baggage compartment.

In London, Frederic and Dominque meet with a Scotland Yard team while you go to see a friend, Jason Lombard. He also helped you when you were working on the stolen painting case in Washington. Jason, a student at Oxford, is spending a school break at home in London.

He's delighted to see you and intrigued by the case. You fill him in on as much as you're allowed to tell. He immediately offers to help you in any way he can.

"Well, the first thing you could do is lead me to the best art dealer in the city," you say. "We'll start there. Information about famous paintings gets around. It's worth a try."

"No problem," Jason replies. "The best art dealer in the city happens to be an old friend of my father's."

Turn to page 19.

You and Pierre travel by train to Milan, Italy, and then to Zurich through the Swiss Alps. It feels like the longest train ride of your life.

"Look at those mountains," you exclaim to Pierre, as they fly past your window. "They're beautiful. I love the sight of snow on them."

"There is glacier skiing high up in the mountains all year round," Pierre tells you.

Go on to the next page.

12

As you watch a group of boarding passengers load skis onto the train's overhead racks, you spot a man carrying two long tubes—just the right size to contain rolled-up paintings. When the porter

asks if he wants to store his packages overhead, he shakes his head.

"He could be our man, Pierre," you whisper.

"Let's follow him," Pierre whispers back.

Go on to the next page.

The train begins to slow down. "We are now approaching Brig, Switzerland," announces a conductor. Everyone with skis gets ready to get off. The man carrying the packages also stands up. He puts on his coat.

You and Pierre stand up and grab your belongings.

The train rolls to a stop and you follow the man off the train and onto a smaller one en route to Zermatt, home of the Matterhorn. At a stop half-way to Zermatt, the man suddenly rises and gets off the train.

"Hurry. Follow him," you hiss to Pierre.

Turn to page 28.

This grabs your attention. "Excuse me, sir, but do you know where these sales will take place?" you ask.

"Yes, one will be at an estate in Scotland, just outside Glasgow. The other is not actually a sale, but a showing. It will be in Oxford."

"What do you mean not actually a sale?" you ask.

"Well, I've heard that a famous painting is to be unveiled at a private reception at one of the colleges in Oxford. Not that the university would have anything to do with a stolen masterpiece, but rumors are that it is a 'famous and priceless work.' You never know."

If you choose to fly to Scotland to follow up on the Glasgow lead, turn to page 50.

If you agree that Oxford is a longshot, but want to check it out anyway, turn to page 35.

16

The plane for the short hop to Jersey—a Mitsubishi turboprop jet—is parked a short distance from the air terminal building. You, Dominique, and Frederic cross the tarmac runway and board. You settle into your seat. Frederic and Dominique sit together across the aisle, two rows forward. Your plan is to watch for any suspicious-looking passengers.

Before takeoff you notice that the man sitting next to you is trembling. "What's the matter, sir? Are you afraid of flying?" you ask him.

"N-no, I am fine."

The takeoff is smooth. But presently you realize that two men sitting three rows ahead keep glancing back at you. Ten minutes later, you see one of them enter the cockpit while the other starts working his way toward you. Suddenly he pulls out a gun! The man sitting next to you leaps to his feet, stumbles across your legs, and heads for the rear of the aircraft. The gunman follows. You remain seated, stunned, while across the aisle, Dominique and Frederic fumble with their seat belts, then spring out of their seats. Frederic draws a pistol, as the two agents rush toward the back of the plane.

Turn to page 30.

"Take them down to the old dungeon and chain them up," the man orders the guards who are holding you and Pierre.

"Hey, we're just tourists!" you plead. "Really. I mean it."

"Hogwash. Besides, you have seen too much for us to let you go." The man turns his back and faces the *Mona Lisa*.

The dungeon is damp and dark, and you wonder how many people once ended their lives in misery here.

"We'll never get out," Pierre says. He is almost crying.

"Yes, we will. You radioed the Sûreté. They know where we are. Don't give up."

You've barely finished speaking when the door to the dungeon opens, revealing two stern-looking men.

"We're agents of the Austrian police," one announces. "You're free now."

"Nice work!" the other says. "We've been after these people for months, but we never had any thing to pin them. They've got international connections, too. Who knows where the *Mona Lisa* might have ended up."

You sigh with relief.

Later, you call Mme. Delavoix. She's ecstatic.

"By the way," she says, "we have just had a call from Mozambique. They want your help in finding an heir to the throne. He has been kidnapped. Are you interested in the job?"

The End

The two of you make your way through the crowded London streets to the art dealer's. As you walk you're struck by how much older the buildings are here than in America. Finally you reach a small shop on a back street.

"Jason, my boy, how nice to see you. What may I do for you?" says a bespectacled old man.

"Mr. Forsythe, this is my friend from America. We're sort of, um . . ." Jason breaks off, appearing to look embarrassed, "sort of interested in the missing *Mona Lisa.* I don't suppose you've heard of anything. . . ."

"Well, the only help that I can give you is to tell you that there are going to be two special, private art sales this week in England. *Very* special, and very private," Mr. Forsythe adds.

Turn to page 15.

Riding the TGV is the train ride of your life. Speeding along at one hundred fifty miles per hour, you feel as though you're standing still. You reach Calais in a matter of hours and get a good night's sleep. The next morning Pierre searches for clues and information in the cafés while you scan the boats in the harbor.

Before long you strike up a conversation with an old fisherman who has docked his boat at this port for over fifty years.

"Has any of these boats arrived in the harbor within the past two days?" you ask casually.

The old man responds in a gruff voice, "You see that small cutter over there? The gray one?"

"Yes."

"Well, she just came in today. Trouble follows that boat. Trouble as gray as its hull. She's a smuggler, I assure you. Whenever she's in port, things go bad. . . . But you didn't hear that from me." The old man ducks his head and walks away.

You look toward the cutter. What attracts your attention, however, is a sailboat in the distance. Alongside it, you can dimly make out a shape.

You find Pierre quickly and bring him back to the docks. "Can you hand me the infrared binoculars?" you ask.

Go on to the next page.

Pierre does so and you gradually focus on the sailboat. The shape you noticed is a small dinghy, and three men are loading cargo onto the sailboat.

You tell Pierre what you see, then say, "Let's split up, Pierre. One of us can check the cutter, the other can check the sailboat."

"Split up?" Pierre echoes. "That's kind of dangerous. How about alerting the police instead? They could check out one boat while we check the other."

You think about Pierre's suggestion. Your friend has a point; it is dangerous to split up. But on the other hand, if you get the police you'll lose a lot of time.

If you take Pierre's advice and call the police, turn to page 41.

If you insist on splitting up and investigating on your own, turn to page 44.

22

After six hours of waiting, Pierre is allowed to enter Austria. By the time you arrive in Vienna, you're both very tired. You drive directly to your hotel, where you're met by members of the Austrian national police. They tell you that Interpol believes the thieves are now on their way to Hungary, heading for a mountain pass some distance from Budapest.

"Can you believe that?" you say to Pierre. "Just six hours and they get away from us. At least we'll get to see a Soviet-bloc country. Sergeant Schnitzler says we can either drive or fly to Budapest and double back to the border. If we drive, we can stay undercover as students. We'll be less conspicuous. But if we fly, we might make up for some lost time. What do you think, Pierre?"

"It's up to you, my friend."

If you choose to fly to Budapest, Hungary, turn to page 84.

If you choose to drive to the nearest border crossing, turn to page 38.

Pierre knows the route to Reims very well, having spent summer vacations there. The drive is an easy one, and you arrive at the port that evening. The next morning, you're up early, and you take your positions along the docks. Three large Sea-link ferries are waiting to leave for England, a trip beginning here on the Vesle River. For two hours you watch the ferries fill with cars and passengers, spotting nothing suspicious.

Shortly before the last ferry's departure time, you notice an unmarked black van drive aboard the ferry. On a hunch, you and Pierre buy tickets and radio the Sûreté to tell them of your plan to board the ferry and follow the van. You also ask for people from Scotland Yard to be waiting across the English Channel, in Dover, England, the ferry's destination.

Pierre parks your car on board, and the two of you get out and begin your search for the van among the rows of cars. Finally Pierre sees it at the end of a row and peeks through the window. He gasps and gestures toward you.

Go on to the next page.

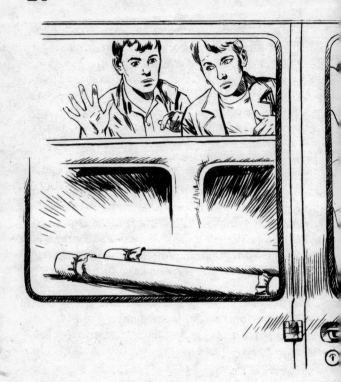

"There are paintings in there! Let's find the people who drove aboard in the van and make an arrest!"

"No," you reply, joining him at the van and looking through the window at the tubes wrapped in brown paper. "We can't be sure that those tubes contain paintings, and besides, we don't have any solid evidence that the van's passengers are thieves. For all we know, those tubes could contain paintings or posters they actually own."

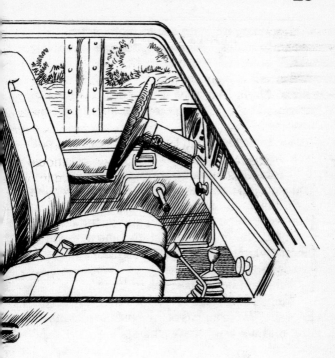

"Well, then let's at least break into the van and look inside the tubes," Pierre insists.

*If you agree to break into the van,
turn to page 48.*

*If you decide to wait until you reach England
before investigating further, turn to page 32.*

"I'm going in," you say to Dominique.

She hesitates. "All right," she says at last.

You enter the apartment.

"Here it is!" you yell.

The *Mona Lisa* in all its beauty. You can't believe your eyes. "It's more beautiful than I ever imagined."

But Dominique isn't paying attention. "What was that noise?" she asks.

"Probably someone in another apartment," you say. You can't take your eyes off the painting.

Suddenly the front door bursts open, and two men knock you and Dominique to the floor.

One of the men shouts something in a guttural language, and Dominique immediately raises her hands in the air.

"Who are you?" you ask in English.

"Hands in the air!" the man shouts in accented English. "We're agents of the Austrian national police, and we want that painting."

Turn to page 40.

"Good!" Sergeant Schnitzler says when you've agreed to pursue the stolen car. He then tells you there is a faster route out of the city. "It will bring you to the road the suspects appear to be heading for—the road to the border crossing. But you *must* hurry!"

The cobblestone roads of Vienna make driving difficult. The Porsche's four-wheel drive helps, but the slippery roads cut down your speed. Finally, you leave the city behind.

The car you're searching for is a Volkswagen Rabbit. You see a number of them on the road before you spot the one you want.

Almost at once, the driver realizes he's being followed. The race is on!

Unbelievably, the Rabbit is every bit as fast as your Porsche.

Must be a racecar with a Rabbit body, you think as you bend over the wheel of your Porsche.

Just as your speed exceeds 200 kph, the screech of tires around curves is punctuated by the sharp *plunk* of bullets hitting your car. There is a blinding explosion as your Porsche slams into a rocky outcropping on a curve.

The End

You have barely enough time to gather your belongings and jump off the train. The first thing you see is a road sign, announcing the distance to Saas-Fee, a small ski town. You assume that is where the man is headed, so you walk up to him and ask him where to catch the bus to Saas-Fee.

"Just follow me. That is where I am going," he answers.

After a fifteen-minute wait, a small bus arrives, and you, Pierre, and the man get on board. The bus eases away, picking up speed on a road that is narrow and hugs the cliffs.

"Look at that. It must be three hundred feet down," you say to Pierre.

"I know, but don't worry. The road is safe as long as we don't go too fast."

In Saas-Fee, you keep your eyes on the man. You follow him around the town, pretending you're tourists looking for a place to stay. No cars are allowed in the town, and it's relaxing to be away from city traffic. Presently the man ducks into a small hotel. You spy on him discreetly and realize he's checking in. At Pierre's suggestion, you get a room in the hotel across the street.

Go on to the next page.

"Pierre, let's get some rest," you say as soon as you're settled. "Why don't you take a nap, and I'll stay on watch at the window. I'll wake you in four hours—unless the man leaves his hotel—then you can go on watch."

"That sounds good to me. We have to get accustomed to the altitude," Pierre answers.

Your watch is uneventful. After four hours, you gratefully lie down on the bed, but less than an hour later, Pierre wakes you.

"Hurry!" he says. "He's leaving his hotel. And he is dressed in climbing gear. He doesn't have the paintings."

"We can follow him," you suggest. "We have our climbing boots. Or we could try to get into the hotel and search his room."

If you decide to follow the man into the mountains, turn to page 49.

If you decide to try to get into his room, turn to page 51.

Moments later a voice comes over the intercom. "This is your pilot speaking. I've been asked to tell you that the plane is now in the control of three men from a terrorist group. Please remain calm. We will be flying to Andorra."

You rack your brain, trying to remember where Andorra is, and finally decide that it's a small principality in the Pyrenees between France and Spain.

You look around impatiently for Frederic and Dominique. What's happened

to them, you wonder nervously. Suddenly shots fill the cabin. A dull thud erupts from the rear of the plane. Smoke and debris follow the explosion. When a large hole appears near the tail section, the aircraft starts to spiral to the ground, almost twenty thousand feet below. Within minutes the plane is nothing but a mass of twisted metal.

There are no survivors.

The End

Upon arrival in Dover, England, you drive ashore, then park a little distance away and watch the ferry unload. At last the van drives off.

You watch as it stops on a side street, and two of its passengers climb out. They get into a small car parked along the side of the road. As the two vehicles speed off toward the north, you and Pierre rush toward the harbormaster's building to meet with the men from Scotland Yard.

Inside you give them the license plate numbers and a description of both the van and the car. They immediately dispatch a car to follow each vehicle. After you fill Scotland Yard in on what you saw in the van, you glance out the window and see the black van driving back down the road. You leap out of your chair. "What's going on? The thieves!"

Detective Sergeant Jacobs, a robust man with a white mustache, tells you not to worry. "I'll dispatch another car and have a helicopter keep an eye on them as well." He radios the helicopter pilot on short-wave. "The black van is heading south on Shore Road about five miles from here. Please follow from the air."

You wonder if the thieves transferred the tubes from the van into the car. Should you take off in your Citröen as backup to the men now tailing the van on the ground? Or, should you wait until the detectives following the car radio in, and let Scotland Yard take care of the van?

*If you choose to follow the van,
turn to page 61.*

*If you decide to wait to see what happens
with the car, turn to page 55.*

Zigzagging between cars, you reach the stairway to the deck above. You scramble up. At the top you realize you'll never reach the main salon without being seen by the two men, who are already on the stairs. Just ahead of you, standing at the railing, is a small group of people.

"We'll join that group," you say to Pierre. "Just act casual."

Out of the corner of your eye, you see the two men searching for you. They look puzzled. Then one of them spots you.

"Ah, old friends," he shouts, grabbing your arm, "We must go back to the van." There's an angry grin on his face and a bulge in his coat jacket. The second man has a firm grip on Pierre. They lead you to the same deserted corner of the ferry that you used to radio the Sûreté. But this time you're pressed against the railing. The dark sea below seems like a very long way down. You're thrown overboard only seconds after Pierre.

The End

You leave Mr. Forsythe, say good-bye to Jason, and go straight to a travel agent to book a flight to Scotland. The flight leaves from Heathrow Airport in four hours, time enough to get in touch with Scotland Yard and to meet with Frederic and Dominique. It is agreed that the agents will remain on watch in London, and Scotland Yard place an undercover team in Scotland. "Careful," Dominique advises you, "these people can be dangerous."

You arrive at Heathrow Airport and check in for your flight. While you are waiting, you see what appears to be a painting wrapped in brown paper on a baggage cart. Casually you step over to the man standing next to it. "What's the painting?" you ask in a conversational tone.

A look of alarm crosses the man's face.

He grabs the painting and quickly heads for the gate to a flight to Vienna. In a matter of seconds, you have bought a ticket to Vienna and are rushing onto the plane after him.

The next thing you know, you're in the air, headed for Vienna, not Scotland.

Turn to page 58.

Jason knows Oxford like the back of his hand, so you ask him to come along with you. You let Frederic and Dominique know where you're headed, but tell them you don't think you'll need help. They agree, sounding as if you're slightly crazy. They do, however, arrange a police contact for you in Oxford.

You and Jason, undercover as students returning to school, arrive at Paddington Station for the train to Oxford.

"Here it is. Hurry up, Jason," you yell. "We're going to find the *Mona Lisa* before dark," you whisper as you find seats. "I can feel it in my bones."

"I hope so," replies Jason, grinning, "but we may need more time than that. The painting is in one of the colleges and we don't know which one. There are forty-two colleges in Oxford University."

"We'll find it. Don't worry," you say.

The train chugs through Reading, and soon you're getting off in Oxford.

A taxi takes you into the center of town. "What a charming place," you say, gazing at the beautiful buildings and lush green hills in the distance. "But you're right, Jason, it may be hard to find the painting. The university is like a small city. We don't know where to start looking."

Go on to the next page.

You start by renting bicycles, and you join the many cyclists pedaling around the campus.

What now? you wonder.

"Hey, look," Jason cries. A crowd of students is gathered by a wall outside Magdalen College. "I wonder what's going on."

Edging through the crowd, you *see* a poster reading:

ART BEYOND BELIEF!
SEE IT YOURSELF
TIME AND PLACE
TO BE ANNOUNCED TONIGHT
AT 8 P.M.

It's now almost eight o'clock.

Turn to page 56.

38

The Porsche lives up to its reputation, and you and Pierre arrive at the border crossing in record time.

You pass through the Hungarian border station quickly and are back on the road in no time at all.

"What now?" Pierre asks.

"I don't know, just keep on driving," you reply. "Interpol will get in touch with us."

A short time later, a report comes over the Interpol radio network, advising all interested parties that the persons suspected of stealing the *Mona Lisa* are now in Hungary, and are driving a small yellow station wagon.

You and Pierre glance at each other, your eyebrows raised. The car in front of you is a yellow station wagon! You follow it all the way to Budapest, where it pulls into a driveway.

Turn to page 72.

Montague leads you out through a side door to the black van. Once inside the van, he insists that you each accept a blindfold.

"Just a precaution, my friends," he says.

You allow him to put the blindfolds on, confident that the men from Scotland Yard will be able to follow the van.

After forty minutes or so, the van stops, and you're led out, blindfolds in place. Up a couple of steps, down two flights of stairs, then straight ahead through dank, damp air. You're obviously underground. The blindfolds are taken off, and you're told to crawl through a small tunnel which leads into a large room. Even though you trust the Scotland Yard agents to find you, as you crawl, you slip off your watch and leave it lying on the floor of the tunnel.

"I can't believe it! You said you dealt with a few stolen paintings, but there are hundreds here," you say to Montague once you're inside the room.

"Unfortunately, very few are real. When a famous painting disappears, we make copies and try to sell them to private collectors as the authentic thing. It's a good business," Montague replies, smiling with pride.

"Can we see some of the 'real' paintings, Mr. Montague?" Pierre asks.

"All in good time, my friend. All in good time. By the way," he says, wheeling toward you, "you dropped your watch in the tunnel." He is not smiling.

Turn to page 108.

It takes a lot to convince them that you're from the Sûreté, but finally, you, Dominique, and the *Mona Lisa* are all safely back in Mme. Delavoix's office in Paris.

"You've done a fine job," she says. "You also helped us to crack an international terrorist group."

"Thank you," you reply modestly.

"I have another case for you, if you want to take it."

"I'd love to," you tell her.

"Very well. Your flight leaves for Africa tonight." Mme. Delavoix is smiling.

"What will I be doing in Africa?" you ask.

"Searching for a lost golden idol. It was taken from a museum in southern France, and was on loan from the people of the Ivory Coast. We must get it back. Our sources say it is in Sierra Leone in the possession of a wealthy German expatriate."

The next morning you're flying over the Sahara Desert. Destination: Sierra Leone, Africa.

The End

You and Pierre hire a boat and are on your way quickly, but the police reach the cutter before you reach the sailboat. You hear sirens as they raid the boat. Soon, however, you see the policemen leave quietly. It looks as if one is even apologizing to the owners. You and Pierre glance at each other.

Your boat glides silently, darkly alongside the sailboat. You creep on board like pirates. Making your way unseen down to the cargo hold, you find stacks of crates labelled "Antiques." You open one of the crates—and stand back in disbelief. You go looking for a stolen painting and find a boatload of weapons!

Turn to page 43.

You turn around to exclaim to Pierre, and realize he's not behind you. In fact, he's not even in the hold. At that moment you hear him scream from the upper deck. A gunshot follows. Footsteps pound toward the hatch of the cargo hold. Someone is coming down the ladder. You swiftly duck behind the cases filled with arms. At any moment you expect a blast of gunfire.

But then a voice says, "No one's here. He must have been alone. We'll dump his body overboard."

Then you hear the investigator climb back up on deck, shove the hatch cover into place, and clamp it closed, for a voyage to unknown parts.

The End

Pierre should be aboard the sailboat by now, you think as you sneak around the cargo hold aboard the cutter, looking for the paintings. To your surprise, you find only cases of wine. You stay below deck and call the Sûreté on your miniature short-wave radio.

The voice that answers your call tells you that the boat Pierre is on is headed for Holland. Pierre found nothing but antiques on board.

You and Pierre manage to make nerve-wracking but uneventful escapes. When you meet up in Calais, you call the Sûreté again. This time you are told that the *Mona Lisa* was found in the possession of a radical terrorist group. The Sûreté rewards you and Pierre for your work, but you feel unfulfilled. Maybe you aren't cut out for detective work after all.

The End

Two hours pass but nothing happens. The students who had gathered for the announcement begin to leave, looking disappointed.

You realize that you'd better check in with the Sûreté. The voice that answers says, "We have found the *Mona Lisa* in Vienna. Please report back to Paris as soon as possible. Mme. Delavoix is anxious to speak with you."

The End

You tell Sergeant Schnitzler you're exhausted and wouldn't be of much help. "I'm sure your efficient police force will catch the suspects before they reach the border," you add. He agrees with you and hangs up.

Ring. Ring. Ring. You're jolted from a deep sleep and grab the phone. "Hello?"

"Sergeant Schnitzler again. We have a new lead on the whereabouts of the painting. Meet me at the Steiffen Plateau in half an hour," he says abruptly.

Within twenty minutes you're crouched with Sergeant Schnitzler and his assistant, Kurt, behind some bushes in a park on a hilltop outside Vienna.

You hear a rustling.

"What was that?" you ask Schnitzler. Before he can answer, three masked men dressed in black jump out of the woods.

Schnitzler scrambles to his feet and is immediately shot in the leg.

"Run for the car!" shouts Kurt.

"What about Schnitzler?" you yell.

"No," gasps the sergeant, "leave me. Run for it."

Kurt opens fire and the three men duck behind a marble fountain.

*If you stay to try and help Schnitzler,
turn to page 3.*

*If you run for the car to escape,
turn to page 62.*

"All right, we'll check the van," you say, "but first let's go up to an outside deck. I want to notify the Sûreté that we may have to make an arrest, and the transmission will be clearer from there."

You and Pierre find a deserted corner of the ferry, where you radio Mme. Delavoix and tell her what's happening.

She warns you to check out the situation carefully, before taking any action. "You'd better be sure the *Mona Lisa* is in that van before you arrest anybody."

You assure her that you'll be very careful, then head back to the lower deck where the cars are parked. You and Pierre creep toward the van's doors. Suddenly, Pierre trips, and falls against the van. The doors fly open, and two men jump out!

If you run for it, turn to page 33.

If you rely on your cover as sight-seeing students, turn to page 57.

"Quick! Put on your climbing boots and let's go," you say. You're already lacing your boots.

"I will be ready in only a minute," Pierre replies. He rummages through his gear. "I am glad that we rested," he adds. "This is a very high altitude. We are going to need all of our strength."

Saas-Fee is surrounded by mountains on all sides except one, where a steep hill drops to the valley below. Pierre pulls you along toward one of the mountains.

"He was heading this way," Pierre tells you. "We're going to have to hurry to catch up."

You find a trail and start up. "I'm glad the trail has leveled out here," you say to Pierre as you hike. "Now we can move more quickly."

You're both panting heavily, but you move as quickly as possible.

"I see him!" Pierre says suddenly. "Look there. Up that little ravine."

You squint up at the hill next to the ravine.

"Pierre, did you see that? Someone else is on that hill, too."

After ten more minutes of fast walking, you're only about a quarter of a mile from the man you're following. There's little cover, so you follow at a distance. Presently the man disappears into what looks like a shepherd's hut.

You train your eyes on the hut. "Now I see *two* other men," you say. "Surely they aren't shepherds. Look, they have skis with them."

Turn to page 116.

"This private sale in Scotland, what else can you tell me about it?" you ask.

"It's to take place tomorrow afternoon in the old castle of the Macdougals," Mr. Forsythe tells you. "Two buyers have been invited to bid for the painting. I'm not sure what painting is being auctioned, but the sale price is expected to be around ten million. That's the rumor in art circles."

This is what you've been waiting for! Surely only the *Mona Lisa* would command such a high price.

"Thank you so much for your help, Mr. Forsythe," you say earnestly.

"Think nothing of it. Good luck!"

Turn to page 34.

Ten minutes later, you and Pierre are walking into the hotel across the street. At the front desk you stop. "Excuse me, sir, but what room is my friend staying in? He's the one who just went out hiking," you tell the clerk.

"Mr. Bennet? He is in room thirteen."

"Thank you," you say. "Did he mention when he was coming back?"

"Yes. Perhaps in three hours. Then he is going to Lucerne," the clerk tells you.

"That's right. We're going to Lucerne together." You turn to Pierre. "Come on," you say. "We'll come back in three hours."

You leave the hotel. Pierre looks completely confused.

"The desk clerk wouldn't have let us go upstairs," you say. "We'll have to sneak up there."

You get your chance when a laundry service truck pulls up, and the driver begins an argument with the clerk. You and Pierre run inside and up the stairs. The clerk never sees you.

Go on to the next page.

You quickly find room 13.

"I hope a credit card really can open doors, like in the movies," you say to Pierre.

Pierre fiddles with the doorknob and credit card. The lock springs open easily. You walk into the room. In one corner, the *Mona Lisa* is stretched out on the floor in plain view!

"Let's grab it," suggests Pierre. "We will go right back to Paris."

"I don't know," you say. "Maybe we should go to Lucerne and see if this guy leads us to the other thieves. There must be more than one. We could catch the whole gang."

*If you choose to take the painting now,
turn to page 80.*

*If you choose to go to Lucerne,
turn to page 102.*

After much discussion, another man comes to the door. It's the man you followed. He recognizes you from the train.

"Don't worry," he says. "We are all going to Zermatt very soon ourselves. You can come with us if you like." He has an anxious look on his face, but he's making an effort to be friendly. "We will be leaving shortly."

Soon the five of you are on your way to Zermatt. One of the men is carrying a roll large enough to hold paintings. You wonder—if it does contain paintings—how they got to the hut. The man you were following didn't bring anything that large with him, you know that. You decide that one of the men must have gone down to Saas-Fee and brought back the paintings while you and Pierre were getting your skis.

Hours later, high on the glacier, you stop for a break. While the men pore over a map, you sneak a peek at the roll. There it is! The *Mona Lisa!*

Turn to page 117.

Time drags as you wait. Finally, about an hour later, Detective Sergeant Jacob's men call in with their report. They've tracked the car to an old manor house in a tiny town about sixty miles away and will wait for backups to assist them.

An hour later you, Pierre, and William and Ian, two detectives from Scotland Yard, pull up across the street from the manor house. Parked down the road are the detectives who pursued the car. They tell you that they tracked the car here and watched the two passengers enter the house. Since then there hasn't been any activity outside the house. Together you decide that they'll continue to watch from the street while the four of you investigate.

Ian and William check around the rear of the house while you and Pierre look around the front. Ten minutes later, you meet in the bushes near the back of the house.

"Did you find anything?" William asks.

"No, but there are many expensive-looking paintings inside the house," Pierre replies. "We saw them through the windows."

"That's good enough for me," Ian says. "Let's go!"

Turn to page 83.

"Impossible," says Jason flatly. "No one would advertise like this if they really had the stolen *Mona Lisa*."

You agree, but are about to say you'd better check it out anyway, when you hear two students talking about the theft from the Louvre. When you move closer you hear one of them say, "We've got it." Then he hurries off.

"I think we should follow him," you tell Jason after you fill him in on what you overheard, "but it's almost time for the announcement."

If you follow the student, turn to page 66.

If you decide to stay where you are, turn to page 45.

As you stand your ground, one of the men yells in French. *"Qui êtes-vous?"*

You understand but respond in English. "Sorry, I don't speak French."

The men relax a little. The second one begins talking with you in English.

"I am sorry to have frightened you. You please must excuse us," he says, smiling.

"My friend, Pete, and I were admiring your van," you say with a wide, friendly grin. "We're on our way to London for a few days."

"Tourists?" asks the man pleasantly.

"Yes," you reply. "We were in Paris last week and had a great time, except for the fact that the *Mona Lisa* was stolen before we got a chance to see it."

"What a coincidence," says the man. "We are art dealers on our way to a show in London. My name is Bernard Montague, and this is my colleague, Samuel Dumond. Would you like to come and see the art show while you are there?"

"Sure!" you reply, as he hands you his card. "We'll be there tomorrow. Thanks, Mr. Montague."

Turn to page 63.

Twenty minutes into the flight, you unbuckle your seat belt and pretend to head for the lavatories, keeping your eyes peeled for the man. You find him sitting alone in a seat near the window and boldly drop down behind him.

That's the last thing you remember until—

"What happened to me?" you ask the stewardess who is waking you up.

"We are now in Vienna," she answers in a lightly accented voice. "All the others have left the plane. You are the last one on board. Are you ill?"

You feel a sharp pain, and put your hand to your temple. Your fingers find a large bump on the side of your head. Now you're on your own in Austria without any clues, except for a strange man with a painting.

The grogginess fades away. The man with the painting! You jump up and dash off the plane. Just as you're getting through passport control you spot the man heading toward the exit to the terminal. You rush after him, and are just in time to see him climb into a car and drive away.

"After that car!" you shout, jumping into the first available taxicab.

Turn to page 112.

Pierre drives through West Germany toward Austria. The road is empty, and, since you're driving on the autobahn, a German expressway, there's no speed limit. Soon you approach the Austrian border.

"Passports, please," the man at customs says.

You hand yours over while Pierre searches his pockets. He becomes more and more frantic.

"I can't find mine!" he tells you at last. "I must have lost it! But I don't see how. I'm sure I packed it."

"Well, you can wait here while we have you checked on," the customs official says, "but that may take all night. What identification do you have?"

Pierre comes up with his driver's license.

The customs official takes it, then enters his small office.

"Why don't you go on ahead without me," Pierre suggests. "Time is important. I will meet you in Vienna."

If you agree to take the car and go on without Pierre, turn to page 87.

If you decide to wait for Pierre, turn to page 22.

You and Pierre run out to your car and jump in. Within ten minutes, you've caught up with the van and the Land Rover occupied by three men from the Yard.

The road is straight and uncrowded, and it's difficult to follow the van without looking too suspicious. You hear the helicopter overhead. Suddenly, the van turns off the road onto a small, winding country lane. The chase is on. Three miles later, you can no longer see the van, but are not worried. You radio the helicopter and ask them where the road leads.

"After about twenty miles it meets up with a large waterway," the helicopter pilot tells you.

"Should we try and stop them now?" you radio the officers ahead of you.

"We'll check with George Winthier, the head of Special Ops," replies one detective. He busies himself with the radio. Finally, he gives you a thumbs-up sign. "We'll try to get them on a traffic violation, if nothing else," he radios you.

Turn to page 79.

62

"Kurt! I'm coming! I'm right behind you!" you cry. But one of the men raises his gun and shoots. It's all over for you.

The End

As soon as you and Pierre are alone again, you radio the Sûreté and report your plan to attend the art show. The rest of the crossing is uneventful. You and Pierre keep an eye on the van and its inhabitants. Montague stays out of sight. He could be an authentic art dealer. He could be a thief. You'll have to keep your eye on him in London.

Finally you land. You drive wearily to London. Overtired from all of the traveling you've been doing, and from the excitement of this mad chase, you fall into an exhausted sleep in the tiny hotel Mme. Delavoix told you to stay in. You sleep soundly, knowing that the Sûreté has arranged with Scotland Yard to follow the van and Monsieur Montague.

They will contact you by radio when necessary.

Turn to page 76.

"Oh, hiking. I'm just out hiking," you reply.

"I think not. I think you were trying to follow me," he says in a voice as cold as ice. He draws a revolver from his parka pocket.

In a desperate attempt to escape, you scramble up a ledge and leap across a narrow gorge. But you misjudge the distance by a couple of inches and plunge one-thousand feet. Your fall to the rocks below seems endless but in reality lasts only a few seconds.

The End

You watch the student turn down a small road. Then, leaving your bikes, you and Jason run to catch up with him. The road zigzags around. After several breathless minutes, you see him enter one of the colleges.

"This is Christ Church College," Jason says, as you follow the student inside. You're close behind as he climbs a flight of stairs and approaches a room just off the landing. The heavy wooden door to the room is open. You hear the murmur of voices.

"Let's go in."

"Right," Jason agrees.

The room is crowded with students talking about art and painters, but you don't see anything suspicious. No one seems to notice your presence. The student you followed is in the midst of the crowd, talking with friends. He seems completely at ease.

As you and Jason turn to leave the room, you notice a package about the size and shape of a painting wrapped in brown paper. Jason follows your gaze and spots it, too, in the far corner in the room.

"Before we do anything else," you whisper to Jason, "let's make contact with Scotland Yard."

Go on to the next page.

The police station is right around the corner from the college. You explain who you are, and the constable on duty introduces you to a heavy-set man.

"Hello. We've been waiting for you," the man tells you. "I'm from Scotland Yard—Detective Inspector Dennis Taylor."

"Glad to meet you, Inspector Taylor." You tell him what you overheard and about the package in the student's room.

Inspector Taylor draws on his cigar. "It doesn't seem likely that the *Mona Lisa* was stolen or purchased by university students, but you never know. It's at least worth looking into."

Turn to page 93.

You and Pierre are to travel by train from Paris to Stuttgart, West Germany. There, you will be met by two members of the Baden-Württenberg State Police, who will arrange for motor transport into Austria.

"Pierre, how much farther is it to Stuttgart?" you ask as the train passes through a station without stopping.

"Only about three more hours," Pierre tells you. "I am going to sleep the rest of the way."

That sounds great to you, and you both doze off until your arrival in Stuttgart.

You wait for Georg and Wilhelm outside the Stuttgart station. A silver Porsche pulls up, and the driver waves to you. As you approach the car, he flashes an ID card. You and Pierre slide into the car, and the driver greets you. "Hi. I'm Georg. This is Wilhelm."

"The Porsche factory is right down the road," Wilhelm adds. "They are waiting for you.

A Porsche! You certainly hadn't expected that!

At the factory, you and Pierre choose a black Porsche 959, the new rally car. It has four-wheel drive and is extremely fast. Georg and Wilhelm wish you luck, and before you know it, you're on the road, driving to Vienna. Your cover—that of carefree students—has been set in motion.

Turn to page 60.

You stop the car and roll down the window. One of the men asks you something.

"I'm sorry," you say, "I don't understand. He switches to English and asks you for a lift to a small airfield about five miles down the road. You look at Pierre and shrug. Why not?

You drive through the woods to the small airfield. There's a twin-engine plane warming up. This is an odd spot for an airfield, you think.

As you slow the car, one of the men leans into the front seat. He's aiming a gun at you.

"Get out of the car and into the plane," he says coldly.

You and Pierre comply quickly.

"We are holding the *Mona Lisa* for ransom," one of the men tells you. "I won't say where. Our little, shall we say, organization, likes to have things to ransom. When we flagged you down, we just wanted a lift to the airport—our car ran out of gas. We certainly weren't expecting to capture such a prize!" He smirks at you. "We know who you are. We saw your picture in the paper last year. So— now we have two more items for ransom."

It's now more than eighteen months since you were kidnapped. Nobody paid your ransom, and it looks like time is running out. In other circumstances, life on a tropical island could be blissful.

The End

You decide to put off contacting the Sûreté until after you talk with Pierre. You go to the top of the Eiffel Tower for your meeting with him. Even in March, the tower is crowded with tourists. But

Pierre is watching the elevator, and he signals casually to you as you step off.

"Quickly. Over here," he says, pointing to an unoccupied corner.

You look at him questioningly.

"I have something important to tell you," Pierre goes on. "I wanted to give you the information in a public place. It is less conspicuous."

You nod, and look at the view of Paris below you, as if you're just a tourist enjoying the sights.

"There is a shipment of stolen art leaving Paris early tomorrow with London as its destination," Pierre says. "My sources think it is a safe bet that the *Mona Lisa* is in the shipment."

You stare at Pierre with amazement. "I've hardly arrived in Paris, and it looks like you've practically solved the case! I'll have to go to the Sûreté, you know. We can't keep this information to ourselves. Do you want to come with me? If not, I'll leave your name out. No one will ever know."

Pierre frowns. "I may be putting my life on the line," he replies, "but I will come."

You call Mme. Delavoix at the Sûreté with the news, but she doesn't sound as impressed as you'd hoped.

"This is the Sûreté you are dealing with," Mme. Delavoix says into the phone. "I do not expect you to change meeting times at your whim. Come to my office right away. We must make plans."

Turn to page 78.

You park a little distance down the street and call the Hungarian Secret Service. You explain who you are and refer them to Mme. Delavoix at the Sûreté. Then you tell the secret service agent about the yellow station wagon and give its location.

"The address you gave us is that of an international trading company dealing in fabric and leather goods," is all the agent tells you. You have a feeling he's not very interested in your information.

You and Pierre return to the "trading company" and park your car across the street. By chance, as you're getting out, you almost collide with two men. You're certain they were in the yellow car earlier. You talk fast.

"Pierre, what shall we do tomorrow?" you ask just so the thieves can hear that you speak English.

"I do not know," Pierre responds, with a quizzical glance at you.

"Well, what do you know? We're tourists from the United States, too," one of the men says. "Where are you from?"

"Washington, D.C.," you reply. "But actually, my friend Pierre is from France."

"Good to meet you two." The man extends his hand. "We thought we were the only English-speaking people in Budapest. Say, how'd you like to have lunch tomorrow?"

Go on to the next page.

"Fine," you reply.

"It'd be nice to talk with another American," the man says. "And maybe you can do us a favor."

"Sure," you say. Now you're the one who's puzzled.

"Meet us here at noon then," calls the man. He and his friend wave to you and Pierre.

You check into a hotel, and telephone the Hungarian police. You're quickly connected with the same agent you spoke with earlier. He seems surprised but interested now, when you tell him about the "American tourists" at the trading company.

Turn to page 97.

Two hours later, you and Pierre have gotten your skis and are almost back at the hut for the second time.

"These skis weigh a ton," you say to Pierre.

"They certainly do," he agrees. "I am glad that you decided to come along with me. I could never have carried them back by myself." Pierre sounds exhausted.

As you approach the shepherd's hut, you enter the woods and leave your packs and skis against a tree. "Remember our plan?" you whisper.

Pierre nods.

You walk right up to the hut and knock on the door.

"Hello? Is anybody here?" you call.

You hear a great scuffling and shuffling from inside.

"What do you want?" barks one of the men. He opens the door a crack and peers through.

"We are trying to hike to Zermatt to go skiing, but I am afraid that we are lost," Pierre says.

"Too bad," replies the man, and closes the door.

You knock again.

Turn to page 54.

You decide it's worth the risk.

"Stop here, quickly," one of the men says suddenly.

You pull the car to a screeching halt.

The men jump out, run into the woods, and return carrying the *Mona Lisa*. You speed off. Ahead you can see the border station, but the gates are closed.

"Go as fast as you can and smash through the gates," Pierre tells you.

But as you crash through the barrier, a hail of machine gun bullets ends your adventures forever.

The End

The next morning—after being awakened at dawn by a phone call—you and Pierre meet with a detective inspector from Scotland Yard. It is decided that plainclothes detectives from the Yard will also attend the art show. You and Pierre are not to arrive at the show until almost five o'clock.

You take the underground, the London subway, to the art show, and find that it's being held in what was once an old warehouse. It now boasts white walls, high-tech lighting, and modern furniture. The crowd at the show is well-dressed and well-to-do. You and Pierre look out of place.

"Hello. I am so glad that you could make it," Bernard Montague greets you as soon as he sees you.

"We wouldn't have missed it for anything," you reply.

"Would you please come with me for a few minutes? I have something to discuss with you."

Out of the corner of your eye you see two men in overcoats standing among a crowd of people looking at a large abstract painting. One of them looks over his shoulder at you. You wonder if they're the men from Scotland Yard.

Turn to page 86.

You reach Sûreté headquarters by four o'clock and are quickly ushered into Mme. Delavoix's office. She looks cross, and says briskly, "You lead the operation. I'll assign two of my agents, Frederic and Dominique, to you."

You wonder about Pierre's role in the case, and at that precise moment, he speaks up.

"Excuse me, Madame," he says to Mme. Delavoix, "but will I be involved? After all, it is I who got the lead."

Mme. Delavoix looks him over coldly, then says, "The Sûreté has its own sources. Please wait outside for a few moments."

After Pierre closes the door behind him, the head of the Sûreté gives you two options: You may work alone with Pierre, or you may work with the two Sûreté agents. You know she is miffed that you decided to meet with Pierre before coming to the Sûreté, but you try to put aside her feelings as you think about the best way to solve the case. Will the lead provided by Pierre's underground connections prove more accurate than the information gathered by the Sûreté's hardened professionals?

If you decide to work alone with Pierre and follow up on his lead, turn to page 82.

If you choose to work with the Sûreté agents, turn to page 5.

With the Scotland Yard detectives in the lead, you follow the van's route as the helicopter pilot reports it. Fifteen minutes later you're right behind the van as it turns down a dirt road, pulls into a field, and stops. The Land Rover jerks to a halt behind the van. You swing in beside it. Overhead is the helicopter. Something nags at the back of your mind, but there's no time to think about it. . . .

"Now!" barks a voice over the radio.

You and Pierre burst out of your car and rush the van. The Scotland Yard detectives rush to your aid. "Come out with your hands up!"

A middle-aged man climbs out of the van. He is shaking badly.

"What is happening?" he asks. Inside the van are a woman and three small children.

Pierre nudges you. "This is a family out for a drive," he mumbles.

You run behind the van and check the license plate. *That's* what was bothering you. The plate number is different from the one you saw earlier.

"Sorry," you say to the frightened family. "We thought you were someone else. It's a case of mistaken identity."

The van with the paintings is probably well on its way to London. You've lost it for now. Oh, well, you think to yourself, perhaps the car from Scotland Yard originally dispatched to follow the van is still on its tail.

The End

"You grab the painting," you say to Pierre. "I'll go out into the hall and make sure the coast is clear."

The hallway is empty.

"It's safe," you whisper. "We'll leave the hotel through the rear entrance. When we get outside, you go through the woods to the bus station."

"Where are you going?" Pierre asks as you run silently down the hall.

"I'm going to get our bags. Then I'll buy a poster that we can wrap the painting in."

In a short while you're boarding the bus. You find Pierre seated in the rear, and join him. The bus winds down the twisting, treacherous road. Suddenly you feel a lurch. The bus begins to tilt. It leans over farther . . . and farther. . . .

"We're going over the cliff!" you scream.

Nobody survives the crash. In the fire that follows, the *Mona Lisa* is destroyed.

The End

In a flash, your two guests rise. Their American accents gone, they begin speaking rapidly. But moments later, the Hungarian Secret Service agents arrive, and the men take off. They disappear neatly.

"Nice going. What happened?" the agent in charge yells at you. "The *Mona Lisa* will never be found now."

"It's not our fault," you scream back at him. "You didn't respond when we opened the basket of food. And why didn't you go after them?"

"No, it is your fault. Somehow you alerted them. They became suspicious. We are taking you back to headquarters right now," he tells you.

At the Secret Service headquarters, you and Pierre are questioned for some time. Gradually you begin to realize that the Hungarian Secret Service didn't want the *Mona Lisa* to be recovered. You never actually learn their motives for impeding the search for the painting. But you do overhear something about international terrorism. You and Pierre are ordered to leave the country.

Late in the afternoon, you're put on a plane to Paris, where you will soon meet up with your family for vacation. You'll never win the acclaim you received for your work in Washington, D.C., last year, but at least you've gotten to see a lot of Europe.

The End

"Okay, Pierre," you say, ushering your friend back into Mme. Delavoix's office. "From now on we're a team. Just you and me."

"Formidable!" he exclaims. "Together we are unbeatable. I know it. Why, the *Mona Lisa* is almost in our hands!" Pierre is excited, despite Mme. Delavoix's obvious dislike for him.

Mme. Delavoix tells you that all police stations have been notified and will give you any help you want. Then she says hurriedly, "We know that almost all of the large-scale smuggling goes through the ports of Calais or Reims. You can take either port. The Sûreté will take care of the other one, in case Pierre's information is accurate. Your cover, by the way, will be that of students on holiday. However, as such, you will be limited to ground transportation—cars and trains, since presumably you would be able to do more sight-seeing that way."

After the meeting you're led into a room where you're given Sûreté credentials and all sorts of equipment: miniature short-wave radios, infrared binoculars and glasses, tape recorders, and cameras. You're then led to the parking lot where a black car, a Citröen, awaits you.

It's yours if you choose to go to Reims, which is only a two-hour drive away, but to go to Calais, which is farther away, you will take a train called the TGV, which is one of the fastest trains in the world.

If you choose to take the car to Reims,
turn to page 23.

If you decide to take the train to Calais,
turn to page 20.

No one answers your loud knocking. You enter the house and look around, but find nothing. The paintings on the walls are valuable ones, but aren't on any list of stolen paintings. Finally, you turn to the large garage behind the house.

The first thing you see is the van! How can that be? you wonder, remembering that it passed the harbormaster's office at Dover, heading in the other direction. But the two paintings wrapped in paper in the back of the van distract you. Frantically, you tear away the paper. Neither painting is the *Mona Lisa,* but you recognize one of them. It's a Goya stolen from a museum in Madrid, and it has been missing for two years. After a thorough second search of the house you find nothing else. But at least you have one stolen painting. The Spanish government gives you a large reward, and you return home with some good stories to tell your friends.

The whereabouts of the *Mona Lisa* remain a mystery.

The End

84

The flight is smooth and uneventful. As the plane begins to descend, you look at your watch. You're arriving fifteen minutes early. "This is the best plane ride I've ever had," you tell Pierre.

Inside the terminal you head for the car rental desk. The only car available is a small Russian Skoda. You make a face. "I guess we've been spoiled by our Porsche."

Two hours later, you've reached the border station and are asking the guards how to find the mountain pass through which Interpol believes the thieves have passed.

It takes several minutes for the guards to understand where it is you want to go. Then one of them tells you to take the left turnoff ten miles ahead and follow the narrow dirt road. You thank him and speed off.

With some difficulty, you locate the road. It's badly rutted and quite isolated. One or two small farms are all that you pass. You drive for fifteen minutes and notice nothing unusual.

Then as you round a bend, you see three men walking toward you. They wave at you, trying to flag you down.

Turn to page 69.

Once you're out of the main room, Montague leads you and Pierre into a small room, and the three of you sit down around a table.

"I work for a firm that sells paintings all over the world," Montague tells you rather abruptly. "At times we end up with paintings that have been stolen, and we have to smuggle them into certain countries. Return them, if you will. Of course, we are well paid."

You are taken aback. You'd never expected him to reveal this much to you.

"We would like to ask your help—as couriers to take a painting back to France for us," he continues.

"Why have you chosen us?" you ask.

"Because you offer the perfect cover," he responds. "No one would suspect two young people on holiday." If only he knew, you think as Montague continues. "You would be doing a service to art and to France. And . . . we will pay you handsomely. What do you say? Will you do it?"

You and Pierre exchange glances. "Yes," you reply. "We'll do it."

"Good. We will leave at once," Montague says.

If you choose to leave with him immediately, hoping the men from Scotland Yard will follow, turn to page 39.

If you try to signal the Scotland Yard team before you leave, turn to page 105.

"All right, Pierre," you say. "I will go ahead. You take the train as soon as you have your papers in order."

You drive off toward Vienna and finally arrive at the hotel designated by Mme. Delavoix.

The phone is ringing as you enter your room. You pick it up, and an officious voice says in English, "Sergeant Schnitzler, Austrian national police. The suspects you are following have stolen a car and are heading east out of Vienna at this moment. Our people are in pursuit, but if the suspects reach the border we will not be able to follow. Can you pursue right now?" You hesitate, and Schnitzler repeats, "Can you pursue them immediately?"

You close your eyes. You're exhausted from the long drive and the delays. And you don't want to attempt anything so dangerous alone. But if you don't agree to pursue the car, the suspects—and the *Mona Lisa*—may never be seen again.

If you agree to pursue the car, turn to page 27.

If you decline the request to pursue, turn to page 46.

As you wait for the Austrian police to arrive, Dominique looks worriedly at her watch.

"Perhaps they have no intention of coming," she says.

"Well, I'll wait for ten more minutes, and then I'm going into the apartment anyway," you say.

Five minutes later, a small black car pulls up to the apartment building. Two men get out and walk over to you. They introduce themselves as members of the Austrian national police. Together you enter the apartment and begin to search. You find nothing except signs that someone broke into the apartment recently. Very recently.

"Well, looks like we goofed," you say, shrugging your shoulders.

"I hope not," one of the Austrians says coldly. "Causing us to enter an innocent person's apartment by giving us false information is a very serious offense."

Suddenly three men with pistols enter the room. "Hands up!" one shouts, then adds with a smirk, "You are too late. The *Mona Lisa* has been removed from the premises and is scheduled to be sold tonight."

As he finishes the other men bind and gag the four of you, then leave. Soon the smell of smoke drifts through the apartment. You hear the crackle of fire coming from the kitchen. Even though Mme. Delavoix knows where you are—any rescue attempt will certainly come too late.

The End

You write a note to Pierre telling him about the important meeting with the Sûreté. Then you leave his apartment.

At the Sûreté office, you're ushered straight to Mme. Delavoix.

"Welcome, my young American friend," she greets you. "I hope you can help us."

"Thank you," you reply. "I think I've already got a lead." You ask Mme. Delavoix if someone could be sent to get Pierre. "He may be able to help us."

"Of course. Anything," she responds.

Go on to the next page.

Pierre arrives soon. He looks impressed at having been sent for by such a highly renowned agency.

Go on to the next page.

Introductions are made, and Pierre tells you and Mme. Delavoix that he's learned a shipment of stolen art is leaving Paris for London tomorrow.

Mme. Delavoix frowns. "We have learned that the painting is being taken to Vienna, Austria," she says.

"So you want Pierre and me to go to Austria?" you ask.

"Yes, and in the meantime, we'll have a couple of other agents look into the London shipment. There are two routes to choose from. You can travel to Italy and then through the Swiss Alps. This is the route that we believe the thieves will take. If you take this route, you must dress the part—skis, hiking boots, you must look like authentic young tourists. It is possible you may track down the thieves, but it could be dangerous. However, if you go straight through West Germany, you will arrive in Vienna before they do, and we will advise the authorities there to expect your arrival. In any case, your cover is that of young students."

If you choose the Italian route, turn to page 11.

If you choose to travel through West Germany, turn to page 68.

You, Jason, Inspector Taylor, and two constables return to the student's room. The door is now closed.

One of the constables knocks on the door.

A student opens it a crack. "Can I help you with something, Constable?" he says nervously.

"We'd like to look around a little. Is that all right?"

Shaking, the student lets you in. As you look around the crowded room you see that the package has been unwrapped. Displayed in one corner of the room is the *Mona Lisa*!

"This is an arrest," Inspector Taylor says tersely. "We're from Scotland Yard. We'll need to hold everyone for questioning."

The student who answered the door starts babbling. Finally, he says, "So, you see, this isn't the *Mona Lisa*. It's a fake. I had it made as a prank."

Silence falls as everyone stares at the student.

You examine the painting closely. "It *is* a fake," you tell Inspector Taylor. "The painting is still damp."

A mixture of relief and anger fills the room. You, Jason, and the police leave. Later that night, on your way back to London, you hear that the *Mona Lisa* is being held for ransom in Vienna by a group of international terrorists.

For now your work is over.

The End

You and Pierre are beginning to wonder where the Austrian police agents are, when two men approach you. After you've all flashed your ID cards, you fill them in on what has happened. You all agree it would be best to split into two teams.

While the two police agents visit art dealers around Vienna, you and Pierre walk through the streets, poking into stores like tourists, but keeping your eyes open for anything suspicious. Finally you spot the bald man who was walking with Bennet in Lucerne! He enters a car rental agency. You and Pierre follow him in.

"May I help you, sir?" the clerk asks the bald man in English. You wonder how he could tell the bald man isn't Austrian.

"Yes, I would like to rent a car for a week. I'll return it to your agency in Rome."

"Certainly," replies the clerk. "Here are the papers. We need your license and credit card. Just sign here." The clerk hands the man several papers and a set of car keys. "Your car is the blue Volkswagen out front. Thank you."

You wait until the bald man is outside, then Pierre steps up to the clerk.

"Excuse me, sir. We would like to rent a car for a week also. We'll be returning it to Rome as well."

The clerk nods. Apparently he sees nothing strange about this.

Go on to the next page.

"Sign here, please. I need your driver's license and credit card," he says. Pierre hands them to him.

"I am sorry, but you are not old enough to rent a car," the clerk says after looking at Pierre's license.

You step up and flash the Sûreté ID card that Mme. Delavoix gave you, and within minutes you and Pierre are in a white GTI, trying to tail the bald man through the streets of Vienna.

You drive carefully, keeping a discreet distance between the GTI and the Volkswagen. Then, just fifteen kilometers outside Vienna, the Volkswagen pulls up in front of a house. You see the bald man go inside, then come out of the house with a tube wrapped in brown paper. He drives away. You follow.

Turn to page 101.

The carabinieri ask you and Pierre to keep an eye out for the men. Hours later, Pierre spots them in a café. But the painting isn't with them! However, when they leave for the Mountain View Hotel, you follow them to their room. The police are with you.

"Let's storm them," decides one of the officers. "On the count of three . . . One, two, *three!*"

You burst through the door and into the hotel room.

"Hands in the air! You're all under arrest," you cry.

The police search for the painting. Within minutes you have the *Mona Lisa* and the thieves. It turns out that they were couriers for an international terrorist group who had arranged the theft. The carabinieri take over the case. That evening a group of people in Vienna are arrested. The next day, more people are arrested in Lucerne, Switzerland.

A few days later you're in Paris when the *Mona Lisa* is returned to the Louvre. A ceremony in your honor is arranged.

"Our country is deeply indebted to you, and we hereby award you the Legion of Honor." The President of France is speaking to you! You can't believe it. What a trip! From that day on, you wear the badge of the Legion of Honor with pride.

The End

"The setup seems perfect," the agent tells you. "The thieves have no idea that you are in fact chasing *them*. Pack a lunch and suggest an 'American picnic.' Go to St. Margaret's Island in the middle of the Danube River. The weather is a bit cool for a picnic, but no matter. We can arrange the arrest there."

"Sounds like a good plan to me," you reply.

"We will be waiting in the woods close at hand, so don't feel nervous," he adds.

"Once you see us open the picnic basket, you can come and arrest the men," you tell him. "That'll be our signal."

The next day, after buying some food, you meet the men, who like the idea of a picnic, and take them to St. Margaret's Island.

After you spread out a blanket, the men begin to talk . . . and talk . . . and talk.

Finally you say to Pierre, "Shall we eat now?"

"Yes, very good," Pierre responds. "Pass me the basket, please."

Turn to page 99.

Pierre slowly opens the picnic basket and re-moves the food. A minute passes. There's no sign of any police.

Go on to the next page.

You catch Pierre's eye and indicate that it's time to put plan B into action. Before you left your hotel, you began to have some doubts. "We are, after all, in a Soviet-bloc country," you told Pierre. You both agreed to run if anything went wrong.

Now you're poised to run across the small bridge to where your car is parked, but Pierre is standing still.

If you choose to run away, hoping Pierre will follow, turn to page 104.

If you stay put, turn to page 81.

Within a few more minutes the Volkswagen has reached what you think is its destination, a large castle high in the mountains. Pierre drives as close to it as he dares, then parks in the woods. Together you approach the castle cautiously.

"Pierre, go back to the car and radio the Sûreté. Find out what you can about this castle and tell them to get in touch with the Austrian police. We may need some backup," you say.

Pierre comes running back in a few minutes. "The castle is owned by an eccentric millionaire," he tells you. "Supposedly he has all sorts of weird connections with political activists and maybe even some terrorist groups."

"Hmm . . ." you say. "I wonder . . . Let's try and get inside now."

Turn to page 106.

"It's a good thing we didn't unpack," you say to Pierre as you dash across the street to your hotel. "We can leave right away and get to Lucerne before Mr. Bennet does. Then we'll watch for him in the train station."

Later that afternoon you and Pierre are in Lucerne awaiting the arrival of Bennet. The late train pulls in, and you see him get off and cross the platform to another train. He's carrying a suitcase and the two long tubes. Walking beside him is a short man whose head is completely bald.

A conductor tells you that their train is bound for Vienna. You buy tickets and still have enough time to call the Sûreté. You're informed that two agents from the Austrian national police wil meet you when you arrive in Vienna, and will help you to trail Bennet.

Hours later, after a tiring train ride, you walk along the platform a few passengers behind Bennet. But suddenly a large group of children cuts through the line of disembarking passengers, and when the crowd thins, there's no sign of Bennet— or of his bald companion.

Frantically you and Pierre race through the station. Finally you catch a glimpse of Bennet at the ticket counter. You step closer and hear the clerk say, "Here is your one-way ticket to Lucerne, sir."

Go on to the next page.

Lucerne! Why is he going back to Lucerne? you wonder. Then you notice that Bennet is now carrying only his suitcase.

"We should follow him," you say to Pierre, "but Bennet isn't carrying the tubes any longer, and I'll bet he gave them to someone here in Vienna."

"We could stay and look around," Pierre suggests. "The two Austrian police agents who are supposed to meet us may have some ideas on where a stolen painting can be sold in this city."

If you choose to follow Bennet back to Lucerne, turn to page 109.

If you choose to stay in Vienna and work with the Austrian national police, turn to page 94.

You dash across the bridge to the spot where you left your car, Pierre following after all. The men are following you, too, but to your surprise, they don't draw weapons, just call you. They sound frightened.

"Help us, please," says one, and you realize his American accent is gone. "We need to leave the country as soon as possible." "We aren't what you think we are. Please, help," adds the other.

You make a fast decision. "Get in quickly," you say. "We're safe for the time being. This car can go pretty fast."

Once you're on the road, you find out that the KGB, the Russian intelligence agency, was trying to get the *Mona Lisa* from the real thieves. "But we're not thieves. We didn't know we *had* the *Mona Lisa*. We were in Lucerne, we ran out of money, and this man offered us ten thousand dollars to be a courier for him. Only later did we realize what we'd gotten ourselves into. If you'll help us, we'll get you the painting. All we want is to escape from Hungary. We're in trouble here."

"Just follow our directions," the other adds.

Turn to page 75.

As Montague leads you to a side exit, you pass the two men in overcoats. You rub your right eyebrow and give them a meaningful glare. In response one of the men rushes up to Montague and whispers in his ear. The men must work for him! Before you know what's happening, a gun is placed against your back.

"Keep walking or else," one of the men says. "We suspected you from the beginning."

Outside you're led to the van. One of the men ties your hands and legs together. The other takes care of Pierre. After driving for about fifteen minutes, the van stops and you're carried into a large warehouse filled with old packing cases. You and Pierre are dumped into one of them. Despite your screams and pleas for help, the lid is nailed shut.

The End

106

You choose the darkest side of the castle and approach cautiously, cringing every time you snap a twig or crunch on a stone. A servants' entrance is unattended and you enter unobserved. Voices coming from a nearby room attract your attention. Moving stealthily, you and Pierre peer into the room. You see an odd collection of tough-looking men and women, and so many weapons the room looks like an armory. But what catches your eye is a painting covered with a tarp. A large man approaches the painting and pulls the tarp off—there is the *Mona Lisa!*

You gasp.

Turning quickly, the man sees you.

"Who are you? What are you doing here?" he yells.

Two other men grab you and Pierre from behind and force you into the room.

"I *said*, what are you doing here?" the man shouts.

"We're lost. We need directions to Vienna," you say. "Nobody heard us ring your bell."

"You are lying!"

Turn to page 17.

108

Your mouth drops open at Montague's statement, but you quickly recover and take the watch from his outstretched hand. "Oh, thanks," you reply. You wonder if Montague is suspicious of you, but he drops the subject immediately.

"You will travel to Paris tomorrow with two paintings hidden in the trunk of your car," he says.

"Where do we take the paintings once we're in Paris?" you ask.

There is no time for Montague to reply.

Five men from Scotland Yard burst into the room.

"Open that safe!" one of the men yells at Montague.

"I cannot. I do not know the combination," he responds.

"Alfred, blast it open," one of them says to an officer with a satchel of equipment.

Within five minutes, the safe is open and three paintings are taken out. You recognize two of them as paintings stolen a few months ago, but you don't see the *Mona Lisa*.

"Where is it?" you demand of Montague. "Where is the *Mona Lisa*?"

Turn to page 8.

You radio your change of plans to Sûreté headquarters before boarding the train to Lucerne. By the time the train reaches Lucerne, it's early morning. You wander wearily through the train station, wondering where to begin your search. Bennet has disappeared.

Then a woman walks up to you.

"Are you with the Sûreté?" she asks abruptly.

"Why do you ask?" you reply.

"My name is Helga Rheinhart. I have been hired to help you out here in Lucerne." She flashes an ID card at you.

"Great," you say with a smile. "We're searching for a Mr. Bennet. Have you heard of him?"

"Of course," Helga replies briskly. "And I can take you to him."

She leads you through town to a pier.

"From here we must travel by boat," she says, ushering you into a speedboat.

It's a very fast speedboat, and you're soon tying up to a dock.

"This is my house," Helga tells you. "Follow me." She walks toward a small chalet.

Turn to page 114.

As your boat draws closer, one of the men lowers his gun. He hails Helga. "Hello, Helga! I am sorry, but I must call the house and receive permission for your young companions to go inside with you."

Helga docks the boat. Then she climbs out, leans toward the men, and whispers confidentially, "These two are close friends of mine. I think that we can use them."

In no time, you're cleared for entrance to the villa. Once inside, you're introduced to several Spanish-speaking men. They appear to be South American. They eye you and Pierre closely and question you in heavily accented English.

"So," says one, looking at you and Pierre critically. "You two think you can smuggle a painting through customs, do you?" He sounds as though he's going to laugh.

"Of course," Pierre replies confidently. "We are young. Nobody would suspect us of doing such a thing."

After much negotiating, you agree to smuggle a painting to Venezuela where you will be paid twenty-five thousand dollars for the job. When you leave the house, you're carrying a long duffel bag with a secret compartment containing none other than the *Mona Lisa*. You, Helga, and Pierre climb into the speedboat and return to Helga's chalet.

You're surprised to find a man waiting on Helga's dock. "Who's that?" you hiss.

Go on to the next page.

"He works for the smugglers," "Helga replies softly. "He's here to make sure we—and the painting—get on the plane."

"Uh-oh," says Pierre.

Your mind races. "Well, this is going to be tough," you say, "but I have a plan. What flight are we booked on?" you ask Helga.

"Air France flight nine-fourteen. It leaves at nine tonight."

As all four of you walk from the dock to Helga's chalet, you shove the painting at Helga. "Here! You take this. I'm going to grab some sleep."

Helga looks surprised at your abrupt tone. But the man who was waiting at the dock smiles. He seems to approve of your attitude toward Helga. Pierre looks confused.

You march purposely into the house, snatch up your pack, and quickly climb the stairs.

When you come downstairs an hour later, the others are sitting around the kitchen table, eating. You join them.

At six o'clock, the four of you are speeding across the water, heading for a point on shore where the man's car is parked. From there you drive to the airport and board flight 914.

"The customs officials did not even look twice at you," the man says in amazement as he sits down next to you, "while I was searched thoroughly. Helga made the right choice when she picked you."

Turn to page 118.

The chase lasts for ten hair-raising minutes and ends when the car your taxi is trailing stops in front of a small apartment building. As the car pulls away, the man enters the building, apparently unaware that you've been following him.

After waiting a few moments, you, too, enter the apartment building. The man is letting himself into apartment 12. Now it's time to contact the authorities.

You use your miniature short-wave radio to contact Sûreté headquarters in Paris. Mme. Delavoix tells you she'll get in touch with the Austrian national police. Something in her voice alerts you.

"Will there be a problem?" you ask.

"Perhaps. One cannot always— I will send Dominique to help you, just in case. My assistant is speaking with Frederic now. Dominique can be in Vienna within four hours. Keep your eyes on that man—and keep us informed of your whereabouts at all times." She cuts the connection abruptly.

You go to a café across from the apartment building and watch the apartment from the café's front window. Night falls. At long, long last you see Dominique get out of a cab and hurriedly pay the driver. You dash to the door of the café and call to her.

Go on to the next page.

When you're both seated at the table by the window, you fill Dominique in on what's been happening. You've just finished when the man emerges from the apartment building.

"Let's go!" you whisper urgently. "We mustn't let him escape."

You follow the man, but this time he's aware of you. He starts to run, slips, falls, then is on his feet running again. He runs down Bergstrasse and you lose him in the tangle of old streets.

"Look, he dropped these," Dominique says, holding up a key ring. "They're probably the keys to his apartment."

You return to the apartment building, wondering if you should go inside now or wait for the Austrian authorities, who haven't shown up yet— if they're even coming.

If you choose to enter the apartment now, turn to page 26.

If you wait for the Austrian national police to arrive, turn to page 88.

"I have spent two years working undercover trying to get to the bottom of a smuggling ring," she reports when you're safely inside the chalet. "I now suspect that this ring carried out the theft of the *Mona Lisa*. But I do not believe they masterminded the robbery. That, I am sure, was the work of an international terrorist group.

"Ten miles away on the opposite side of the lake, the smugglers have a large villa which is heavily guarded. I will be able to take you there because I have earned their trust," she says in her nonchalant style.

"Well, then let's get going," you reply eagerly. "The sooner we get to work the sooner we'll recover the painting."

"Not so fast. You two need some rest and I must brief you on how you are to act once we are inside their villa," she says.

Hours later, you, Pierre, and Helga board the speedboat and set out across the lake.

You scan the shore for the villa. When it comes into view, you decide that it is the most beautiful home in the world.

Then you see the three men standing on the dock with machine guns.

Turn to page 110.

116

You and Pierre wait until the two men have followed the first one into the hut. Then you decide to sneak up to the hut and try to hear what's going on.

A few more minutes of fast hiking bring you to the woods behind the hut.

"If they should hear us," Pierre whispers, "we will just pretend that we are lost hikers."

"Okay," you agree. "Let's wait here for a few minutes and then move closer."

The door to the hut opens and one of the men comes outside with a gun. He checks the skis nervously, then goes back into the hut.

"Pierre," you say, "I just realized something. Those men are probably going to go somewhere on skis. One of us should go back and get our skis or we won't be able to follow them."

Pierre groans. "But, why follow them? We can't have them arrested; we have no proof. The painting is still at the hotel."

"I don't want to make an arrest, I just want to see where they're going. Look, I know you don't want to go back to the hotel, but we may need the skis."

"If I go alone it could be dangerous for both of us. I do not want to split up. There is safety in numbers, you know," Pierre answers.

If you insist that Pierre go back alone, turn to page 4.

If you decide that you should go back with Pierre, turn to page 74.

Somehow, you manage to say nothing about your discovery, even to Pierre. The five of you strap on skis and descend in swooping arcs to the valley separating Saas-Fee and Zermatt. You end up at a narrow, seldom-used dirt road—more of a cart track than a road.

"Here's our car. From here we can drive almost all the way to Zermatt," one of the men tells you. He looks uncomfortable, but adds, "It is not far and saves much time."

After a twenty-minute ride you arrive in Zermatt. A short walk brings you to a cable-car station.

"Here we leave you," says the man from the train.

"How will you get to Italy from here?" you ask.

"We take the cable car over the Klien Matterhorn," he replies, "then down to Cervinia."

"Thank you so much for your help," you say to the men.

"No problem. It was our pleasure," says the man from the train.

You wait until the men are well out of sight, then give your startling news about the *Mona Lisa* to Pierre. You jump on the next cable car and take it to Cervinia, where you contact the Italian police, the famous Carabinieri.

It doesn't take long to get their help. After all, the *Mona Lisa* was painted by an Italian!

Turn to page 96.

You're less than an hour into your flight, when the stewardess comes by and offers you a soft drink. When she passes it to you, she gives you a quick wink. There is a note written inside the napkin she hands you. It reads simply:

"All set. Pilot will land in Paris."

Ten minutes later, the pilot announces that the plane is experiencing engine trouble and an emergency landing will be made in Paris. The man next to you looks uneasy, but you calm him down. The plane lands and everyone is ordered off. As you walk off the plane with Pierre, Helga, and the man, agents from the Sûreté surround you and place the man in handcuffs. Pierre and Helga look at you, then Pierre says, "You didn't sleep—you radioed the Sûreté!"

The smugglers in Lucerne are arrested as is a group of terrorists in Vienna. In France you're a national hero. You can't even walk down the street without people calling to you and congratulating you.

The End

ABOUT THE AUTHOR

RAMSEY MONTGOMERY is a student at the University of Vermont. He has also studied at Edward Greene's, Oxford, England, and is a graduate of the Green Mountain Valley School. A former ski racer, he enjoys foreign travel, mountains, wind surfing and reggae music. In the summers, he works as a carpenter. This is his first Choose Your Own Adventure book.

ABOUT THE ILLUSTRATOR

GONZALEZ VICENTE was born in Salamanca, Spain, in 1933. His work has appeared in many books and periodicals throughout Europe and the United States. *The Mona Lisa is Missing!* is the first Choose Your Own Adventure book that he has illustrated. Mr. Vicente currently lives in Barcelona, Spain.